FEB 1 9 2008

Truman's Loose Tooth

To the little boy, Truman,
who inspired this book,
and to my own children,
Lynnea and Gavin,
who inspire me everyday

Truman's Loose Tooth

Story by Kristine Wurm

Pictures by Michael Chesworth

Spirited Publishing, LLC
Appleton, Wisconsin

Spirited Publishing, LLC
P.O. Box 1796
Appleton, WI 54912-1796
TEL 1-920-419-3340
www.spiritedpublishing.com

Library of Congress Control Number: 2005903970
Truman's Loose Tooth/by Kristine Wurm & Michael Chesworth

First edition, 2006
ISBN: 0-9768513-0-X   ISBN 13: 9780976851301

Printed in China.

Book design by Michael Chesworth and Kristine Wurm.

10 9 8 7 6 5 4 3 2 1

Truman is a six-year-old boy in Mrs. Baker's first grade classroom. He sits quietly at his desk, like he does every day.

He comes home after school and enjoys a snack, like he does every day.

He plays in the backyard with his best friend, like he does every day, but. . . .

Today was different. Just as he was ready to head down the slide, like he does every day, he noticed his tooth did something *strange*.

His tooth moved a little when his tongue touched it.
He checked it with his finger to be sure.
Yep! It wiggled!

Truman wasn't sure if he could slide anymore. He felt a little woozy.
His friend, Alec, yelled, "Come on, Truman, move!"

Truman wasn't sure whether he could speak with this wiggly tooth.
He spoke very carefully and was able to get out, "Ma-ma-my tooth is wiggly."
"What? Your tooth is wiggly!?" Alec shouted.
"Ah, yeah," Truman muttered.
Alec never had a wiggly tooth before. "Let me see!" he said.

Truman thought he better tell his mom. He wondered what she would say, and what might have to be done about this.

Truman's stomach started to hurt.

Truman's mom was making dinner.
"Mom," Truman said.
"Yes," she replied.
"My tooth is wiggly," he confided.

She laughed. "Really?" she said.
She seemed excited. "Let me see."
He showed her.

"Oh my goodness!" she said. "Can I try?"
Truman removed his finger from his mouth.
Truman's mother was elated. "Truman, your
tooth is going to fall out soon!" she said.

Just then, Truman's older brother, Tanner, and his father arrived home.
"Truman's tooth is wiggly," said his mother.
"Really?" said his father.
"Cool," said his brother.

"I could help you get it out, Truman," Tanner smiled and hit his fist into his other hand.

"No, the best way to remove it is to tie a string to your tooth and a door handle. When you shut the door quickly, out comes the tooth," said his father. Truman's eyes became as big as golf balls.

"No," said Truman, "no one's touching my tooth. It's fine."
"Yes," said his mother, "it'll fall out on its own."

Truman was relieved until his mother called out that it was time to eat. *Eat? How am I going to eat?* he thought. Truman tried to eat as carefully as he could. "May I be excused?" Truman asked his parents, "I'm not feeling well." Truman's parents allowed him to rest in his room.

Truman began to wonder when his tooth was going to fall out. *What if it happens when I'm eating, and I swallow it. . . . or what if I'm asleep, and I choke on it?* Truman thought. He decided he had to think of something else. He turned his TV on quietly and quickly fell asleep.

He woke up, got ready for school and ate his breakfast, like he did every day.

He sat quietly in the second row of Mrs. Baker's first grade class, like he did everyday. Soon Truman forgot about his wiggly tooth until . . . .

He was biting on his pencil while trying to figure out a math problem, like he always did, when his pencil suddenly slipped. His tooth flipped out of his mouth, hit his desk and rolled across the floor.

Truman was stunned. He quickly bent over to not lose sight of his tooth.
It tumbled under Amber's desk where it was stopped by her shoe. Truman quickly and
carefully picked up his tooth.

Mrs. Baker asked him what was going on. He told her that his tooth fell out. She congratulated him and gave him an envelope to place his tooth in. She carefully sealed it with tape, so that the tooth would not be lost on the journey home in Truman's backpack.

Truman suddenly felt much older than he had. Everyone seemed to notice his missing tooth and treated him like a bigger kid. Though it was still strange seeing himself with his tooth missing, he liked that he joined the ranks of the kids who have lost a tooth before.

Truman's family was happy that his tooth fell out and told him that he should place it under his pillow for the Tooth Fairy. The Tooth Fairy, he was told, would give him money for his tooth. Truman liked to have money, but he had become very fond of his tooth. He decided to spend the evening looking at his tooth and showing it to others before selling it to the Tooth Fairy.

That night, Truman placed his tooth back in the envelope and tucked it neatly under his pillow. He began to think of whether he would save the money he would receive the following morning, or whether he would spend it on a new Fast Wheels car.

Truman awoke the following morning and almost forgot to see if the Tooth Fairy had come for his tooth. He quickly lifted his pillow and found a dollar bill. Wow! Truman ran to show his brother, mother and father what the Tooth Fairy had paid him.

After that, Truman went to school, sat quietly in his desk in the second row of Mrs. Baker's first grade classroom, . . .

. . . ate his snack after school, . . .

. . . and played with his friends, like he did every day until . . .

Yep!